First published in the United States, Great Britain, Canada, Australia, and New Zealand in 2015
by NorthSouth Books Inc., an imprint of NordSüd Verlag AG, CH-8005 Zürich, Switzerland.

Distributed in the United States by NorthSouth Books Inc., New York 10016.
Library of Congress Cataloging-in-Publication Data is available.

ISBN: 978-0-7358-4156-7
Printed in China by Leo Paper Products Ltd., Heshan, Guangdong, February 2015.
3 5 7 9 • 10 8 6 4 2

www.northsouth.com

FSC
www.fsc.org
MIX
Paper from
responsible sources
FSC® C020056

Mr. Squirrel
and the
Moon

by **Sebastian Meschenmoser**

North South

One morning Mr. Squirrel woke up
because the moon had fallen onto his tree.

The moon was as big and round and yellow as it had always been, but why was it lying on his tree? Perhaps it had been stolen and the thief lost it?

If someone came looking for it now and
found it . . . here, with him . . .

they would think he was the thief.
He'd be arrested and thrown in prison. . . .

He had to get rid of the moon!

The next morning hedgehog woke up because the
moon had fallen on his back and had got stuck.

Fortunately, Mr. Squirrel was nearby
and was able to help him.

"The moon has fallen on your back and it's stuck. And the awful thing is, it's been stolen! Suppose someone finds us with it?"

They had to get rid of the moon!

Then a billy goat arrived.

He saw the moon and butted it
with his horns.

With the moon stuck on his horns . . .

the hedgehog stuck on the moon . . .

and Mr. Squirrel hard on his heels . . .
the billy goat charged at a tree.

Bang!

Perhaps, Mr. Squirrel thought, he wouldn't get arrested. He could explain what had happened, and the holes in the moon could be repaired.

The next morning the billy goat woke up because the hedgehog, who was still stuck on the moon, complained that it was starting to smell. That was not a good sign. . . .

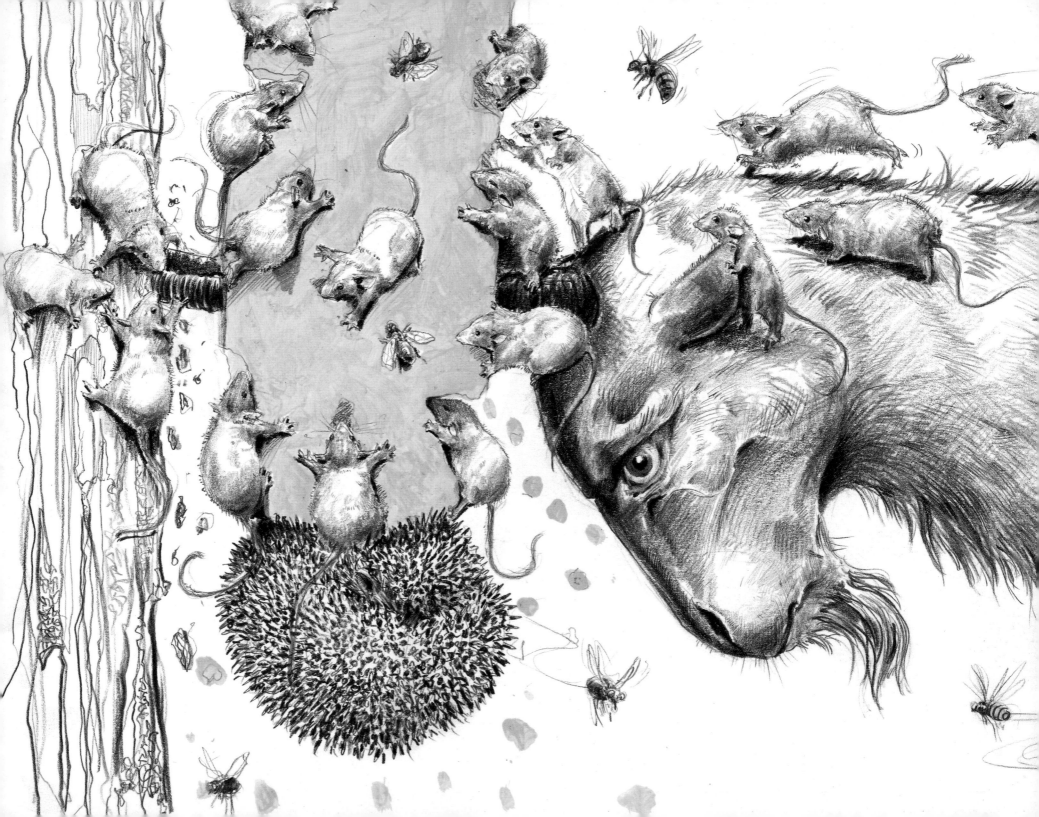

The billy goat was free . . .

the hedgehog was free . . .

the mice had a good meal . . .

but the moon was ruined!

They had to get rid of the moon!

The best thing would be to send it back to the sky
where it belonged.

Now that the moon was back in the sky, Mr. Squirrel thought it would soon be its old self again.